Mimi
the Laughter
Fairy

Join the Rainbow Magic Reading Challenge!

Read the story and collect your fairy points to climb the
Reading Rainbow at the back of the book.

This book is worth 5 points.

To Lowena and Iona

Special thanks to
Rachel Elliot

ORCHARD BOOKS

First published in Great Britain in 2016 by The Watts Publishing Group

3 5 7 9 10 8 6 4 2

© 2016 Rainbow Magic Limited.
© 2016 HIT Entertainment Limited.
Illustrations © Orchard Books 2016

HIT entertainment

A CIP catalogue record for this book is available from the British Library.

ISBN 978 1 40834 897 0

Printed and bound in Great Britain by Clays Ltd, Elcograf S.p.A.

MIX
Paper from
responsible sources
FSC
www.fsc.org
FSC® C104740

The paper and board used in this book are made from wood from responsible sources

Orchard Books
An imprint of Hachette Children's Group
Part of The Watts Publishing Group Limited
Carmelite House, 50 Victoria Embankment, London EC4Y 0DZ

An Hachette UK Company
www.hachette.co.uk
www.hachettechildrens.co.uk

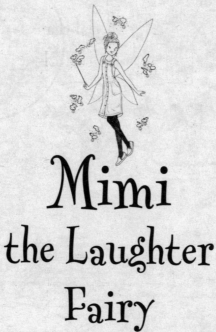

Mimi
the Laughter
Fairy

by Daisy Meadows

ORCHARD

www.rainbowmagic.co.uk

Jack Frost's Spell

The Friendship Fairies like big smiles.
They want to spread good cheer for miles.
Those pests want people to connect,
And treat each other with respect.

I don't agree! I just don't care!
I want them all to feel despair.
And when their charms belong to me,
Each friend will be an enemy!

Contents

Mr Twinkle's Tumble

Kirsty Tate was spinning her way across the park, her arms outstretched as she soaked up the early morning sunshine. It was making the dew sparkle on each blade of grass, and it was shining on the golden hair of Kirsty's best friend, Rachel Walker.

"I wonder what Jen and Ginny have planned for us today," said Rachel, skipping along beside Kirsty.

It was their third day on Rainspell Island, the beautiful place where they had first met – and where they'd had their first fairy adventure! They had joined the Summer Friends Club, a holiday play scheme for children staying on the island, and the club met in the park every morning.

"We've already played football, had a water-balloon fight and painted a mural," Kirsty remembered. "I'm so glad we joined the club."

They reached the tepee-style tent where the club was based and stepped inside. Oscar and Lara, two of their newest friends, dashed over to them.

"Good morning!" said Lara, a big smile on her face.

"Do you know what we're doing today?" Oscar asked.

"We have no idea," said Rachel, with a grin. "It looks as if we're about to find out, though!"

Jen and Ginny, the teenage best friends who ran the club, were beckoning everyone to gather around them. They looked as if they were about to burst with excitement.

"Today we have something really fantastic for you all to enjoy," said Ginny. "We're going to watch a special performance by Mr Twinkle himself!"

Everyone gasped and squealed. Mr Twinkle was the funniest, most famous magician on TV. Like all the others in the club, Rachel and Kirsty

watched his show every week.

"I can't believe we're actually going to see him *in real life*!" Oscar said in a breathless voice. "When I grow up, I want to be just like him and make everyone laugh!"

"Where's the performance going to be held?" Kirsty asked.

"Right here in Rainspell Park," said Jen, with a smile. "We have to wait for him on the steps of the fountain square. I thought you could all race each other to see who gets there first. Ready? Steady! Go!"

Everyone sped out of the tent and sprinted across the grass to the fountain in the middle of the park. A girl called Anouk won the race, and everyone gathered around to congratulate her.

Then they each found a place on the steps to sit and wait for Mr Twinkle.

"My heart's thumping," said Rachel. "I don't know if it's because of running fast or because I'm so excited!"

"There he is!" Kirsty exclaimed, jumping to her feet.

Riding towards them on a unicycle was a very strange-looking man indeed. He was wearing a long purple cape covered in sparkly stars, and a black top hat almost as tall as he was!

"It's so amazing to see him in real life!" said Rachel.

Mr Twinkle waved at the children, his sparkly cape flying out behind him and a magic wand held high in his left hand. The children clapped and cheered, but as he reached them he started to wobble. He zigzagged left and right, his arms waving wildly, but it was no use. *CRASH!* The unicycle shot into a nearby bush and Mr Twinkle landed on his bottom, all tangled up in his magnificent cloak.

Rachel and Kirsty burst into laughter, but no one else seemed to see the funny side of it.

"He's better when he's on TV," Oscar said under his breath.

The other children had stopped clapping. Mr Twinkle jumped to his feet, pulled off his hat and swept a deep bow. Then he waved his magic wand over his hat and pulled out a flower.

"Look at this beautiful bloom!" he cried, holding it up in front of the children. "Take a sniff!"

Everyone leaned forward, and a stream of water squirted out of the flower and straight into their faces!

Rachel and Kirsty were helpless with giggles, but still the other children weren't amused.

"Why aren't you laughing?" Kirsty asked Lara.

"I'm not really in the mood for jokes," said Lara.

"I'm all wet," Oscar complained.

"It's only a few tiny drops of water," Rachel said, trying to make him see the funny side of it.

But Oscar and Lara shook their heads.

Rachel and Kirsty exchanged a worried glance.

"I have a terrible feeling that I know exactly why people aren't laughing," Kirsty whispered into her best friend's ear. "It's because of the Friendship Fairies' magical objects!"

A Gaggle of Grumblers

On the first day of their holiday, the girls had met the Friendship Fairies. Esther the Kindness Fairy, Mary the Sharing Fairy, Mimi the Laughter Fairy and Clare the Caring Fairy had whisked them away to a magical tea party in Fairyland. Everything was perfect, until Jack Frost and his naughty goblins had gate-crashed the party and stolen the Friendship Fairies' magical objects. The Ice Lord had thrown the objects to his goblins, and sent them to hide in the human world.

Rachel and Kirsty had managed to get back Esther's heart brooch and Mary's yin and yang charm, but two of the magical objects were still missing.

As they watched everyone frowning at Mr Twinkle, Rachel and Kirsty knew exactly why the other children didn't feel like laughing. It was because Jack Frost still had Mimi's magical happy face pendant!

"The Friendship Fairies need their magical objects to keep all friendships strong and happy," said Rachel, remembering what their fairy friends had told them.

Kirsty nodded. "One of my favourite things about being best friends with you is laughing and having fun together. But until Mimi gets her pendant 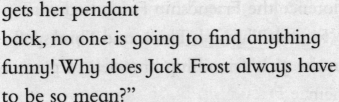 back, no one is going to find anything funny! Why does Jack Frost always have to be so mean?"

The girls looked back at Mr Twinkle. He was still trying to make his audience laugh, but everything he did seemed to make them more grumpy.

"Jack Frost is just thinking about himself," said Rachel. "He ordered the goblins to find some friends for him, remember? He said that if he has lots of friends, he can boss them about and be super-powerful."

"But friends don't boss each other around," Kirsty said. "Oh, Rachel, thank goodness *our* friendship isn't being affected by the missing magical objects!"

Luckily, Kirsty and Rachel's old friend, Florence the Friendship Fairy, had cast a 'Friends Through Thick and Thin' spell on the girls' friendship bracelets to protect them.

"Not yet," Rachel agreed. "But Florence said that the spell won't last long if the fairies don't get their objects back soon. We have to keep looking."

Just then, Mr Twinkle raised his voice.

"I know what'll cheer you all up!" he exclaimed. "New clothes are always a treat. I'm going to magic up a brand-new tie for myself. Get ready to be amazed, boys and girls!"

Mr Twinkle waved his wand over the hat, but the wand suddenly flopped like a piece of limp celery. With a confused expression, Mr Twinkle pulled an enormous cream pie out of his hat, instead of a tie.

"Now, that's not right," he said, scratching his head and looking puzzled.

Rachel and Kirsty held their sides with laughter, but the other children just shrugged. Jen raised an eyebrow at Mr Twinkle, and he grinned at her.

"There's only one thing to do with a pie like this," he said. "It's just begging to be thrown! Cream pies are supposed to end up on people's faces."

He took one step towards her, and then another. He raised the pie and took aim.

"Don't you *dare*," said Jen, who didn't look amused at all.

She backed away, but Mr Twinkle just kept coming towards her, faster and faster, until he was chasing her around in a wide circle. Rachel and Kirsty thought it was funny at first,

until they saw how annoyed Jen looked.

"Stop it!" she shouted at him. "This is silly!"

Mr Twinkle's shoulders slumped.

"But I *am* silly," he said in a miserable voice. "That's what I *do*. People usually love it."

"Not today," Jen snapped.

Mr Twinkle put the pie down on the ground next to Rachel and Kirsty, climbed onto his unicycle and rode away.

"Poor Mr Twinkle," said Kirsty sadly.

The other children were busy grumbling about how Mr Twinkle wasn't funny, when Rachel noticed something peculiar. The cream pie seemed to be glowing. She leaned closer, and saw tiny sparkles glittering on top of the cream.

"Kirsty," she whispered. "I think something magical is about to happen!"

Goblin Antics

Rachel and Kirsty stood in front of the pie so that none of the other children could see what was happening. The girls were always careful to keep the fairies a special secret.

The cream at the centre of the pie seemed to lift into the air, and Mimi the Laughter Fairy fluttered from the middle.

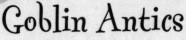

Mimi was wearing a simple denim dungaree dress with navy tights and white pumps. A swirl of cream from the cake was sitting on top of her red-brown hair, like a funny hat. Cream had also caught on her shoulders like a cosy cape, and there was even a dot of cream on the tip of her nose.

Rachel and Kirsty couldn't help giggling.

"It's not funny," said Mimi, looking cross.

The girls stopped laughing immediately, and Mimi sighed.

"I'm sorry," she said. "I'm the Laughter Fairy, but even *I'm* not laughing and keeping things light today. I must get my magical smiley-face pendant back from the goblins before the Fairyland Funny Show tonight, but I have no idea how. Please, will you help me?"

Rachel and Kirsty nodded at once.

"Of course we will," said Kirsty. "What's the Fairyland Funny Show?"

"It's usually one of the best nights of the whole year," said Mimi, looking anxious. "All the fairies tell jokes and perform tricks to make each other laugh. But without my pendant, the show will be a disaster and friends will never laugh together again!"

Just then, Lara let out an excited yell and pointed along the path. Three more magicians were riding towards them on unicycles. They were all dressed a bit like Mr Twinkle, with green capes and green top hats to match. They were much more wobbly than Mr Twinkle, and kept bumping their unicycle wheels together and knocking each other off.

"I'd better
hide," said
Mimi, slipping
into Kirsty's
pocket.

Rachel peered
at the magicians
as they got closer.

"They're wearing an
awful lot of green," she said.

"Yes, and they have big feet and long
noses," added Kirsty. She gasped. "Oh,
Rachel – they're goblins! Do you think
they might be the ones who have Mimi's
pendant?"

"I bet they are," said Rachel. "That
must be why they've dressed up like Mr
Twinkle – they want to have the fun of
making everyone laugh."

One of the goblins stood up on his
unicycle, waving his arms as he tried
to keep his balance. Another stood on
his head and used his hands on the
pedals. The third lay on his stomach
with his arms and legs splayed out as if
he were flying. They all looked so silly
that even Rachel and Kirsty had to smile
at their antics.

"Whichever goblin makes the other children laugh *must* be the one with Mimi's magical smiley-face pendant," Kirsty said.

But the other children were all still looking grumpy. The girls watched them closely, but they couldn't see even a flicker of a smile. Not one person was laughing.

One by one, the goblins jumped down from their unicycles and pulled out green magic wands.

"Now for some magic!" the tallest goblin declared. "Get ready, pesky humans – er – I mean, boys and girls!"

He waved his wand around his head and nearly knocked his hat off, but there was not a single giggle from the audience.

*"Abracadabra!
Stinky-winky!
Fill this fountain
With a green-slime drinky!"*
"That's a terrible rhyme," said Rachel.
"It's a terrible spell, too," Mimi added.
"Thankfully, it won't work. The goblins

don't know how to do magic."

The goblin was staring eagerly at the fountain. When nothing happened, he threw his wand down and jumped on it.

Next, the other two goblins held their wands up in the air.

"On the count of three, we will cast a spell to turn the trees into balls of green wool!" the smallest goblin squawked.

"One . . . two . . . THREE!"

The goblins tapped their wands on each other's nose, and several balls of green wool dropped out from under their capes. The audience groaned.

"Rubbish!" called Oscar.

"Cheats!" Lara exclaimed.

"I can't understand it," said Kirsty. "Surely one of these goblins must be hiding Mimi's magical object? Whoever has the pendant should have the audience in stitches!"

"Something must have gone wrong," said Mimi.

"Mimi, could you turn us into fairies?" said Rachel. "We'll have a better chance of finding out what the goblins are up to if we can keep out of their sight."

Jen, Ginny and all the other children were still staring at the goblins, who were now performing a peculiar dance routine that involved kicking their legs up high and banging their wands together as hard as they could. No one saw Rachel and Kirsty slip away to hide behind the fountain. As soon as they were sure

that no one was watching them, Mimi
fluttered out of Kirsty's pocket and
tapped the girls with her wand. At once
they felt the familiar thrill of their wings
unfurling as they shrank to fairy size.
Suddenly, the world
seemed bigger
and brighter.

"Everything
looks a little
bit more
beautiful
when we're
fairies," said
Kirsty, twirling
around in a few
sparkling drops of
water that splashed out from
the fountain.

Rachel looked up at the fountain too, and saw something interesting. There was a little platform at the top, almost hidden by the water that poured out around it.

"That's the perfect hiding place," she said. "From there, we might be able to see which goblin has the pendant."

Hand in hand, the three fairies zoomed up and perched at the top of the fountain. Through the tumbling water, they were able to see everything.

The goblins finished their show, but no one in the audience clapped. Looking cross, the goblins grabbed their unicycles and dragged them around to the other side of the fountain. They sat down on the dusty path and glowered at each other.

"That was a disaster," said the smallest goblin. "I blame Jack Frost."

"Me, too," said the middle goblin, pulling a stray ball of green wool from under his armpit. "If only he hadn't

snatched that magical pendant, everyone would have been crying with laughter."

"I don't know why he wants it, anyway," added the tallest goblin. "Jack Frost doesn't *like* making people laugh."

Kirsty drew in her breath sharply.

"That's *it*!" she whispered. "I bet Jack Frost has taken the pendant because he wants to perform at the Fairyland Funny Show. If he has the pendant, everyone is sure to think he's the funniest act, and he'll win."

"And Jack Frost *loves* winning," Rachel said with a groan. "Mimi, there's no time to lose. Jack Frost is going to cheat, and that will spoil the whole show. We have to go to Fairyland and stop him!"

Bad Jokes!

Before Rachel had finished speaking,
they had arrived in Fairyland in a swirl
of magical sparkles. They looked around
and saw that they were in the garden
of the Fairyland Palace. The lawn was
dotted with picnic rugs and deckchairs,
where lots of fairies were sitting facing
a little stage, complete with a red velvet

curtain. Mimi led Rachel and Kirsty to
stand in the left wing of the stage, just as
the Showtime Fairies ran onto the stage
from the right.

"Welcome to the Fairyland Funny
Show!" called Isla the Ice Star
Fairy. "We're so excited to present –
WHOOPS!"

She squealed as she stepped on a
banana skin and skidded across the stage.
Madison the Magic Show Fairy grabbed
the microphone as Isla slid past.

"We've got jokes, sketches and tricks," she announced. "But don't worry – I'm sure the whole show will go according to plan – OOOH!"

The microphone jumped out of her hand as if it were as slippery as soap! Rachel and Kirsty spluttered with laughter, especially because Isla was still sliding around on the banana skin behind Madison. One by one, the Showtime Fairies started to do cartwheels across the stage, but their legs got tangled until they all ended up in a great big cartwheel made of seven fairies.

It spun into the air and then twirled downwards and landed with all the fairies *upside down.* The fairies flipped over backwards and bowed – *with their backs to the audience.* Rachel and Kirsty howled with laughter and clapped until their hands were sore, but none of the fairies on the grass so much as smiled.

"No one's laughing," shouted a rough voice. "You're not funny."

Everyone looked around, trying to see who was shouting. Then a movement above the stage caught Rachel's eye. She gasped as she saw a huge, frosted-blue glitter ball coming down slowly, held by a thick chain. It was decorated with golden smiling faces. Two goblins were standing on top of the ball, clinging to the chain and wearing enormous

pointing-hand gloves.
One said,
"Jack
Frost is so
funny ..." and
the other said
"... I can't stop
laughing!"
The goblins
were
giggling
hysterically,
their cheeks
pink and
their eyes wet
with tears of
laughter.

"*I'll* show you what's funny!" the rough
voice went on.

As the glitter ball
touched the
stage, it
opened to
reveal
Jack
Frost. He
stepped
out of the
ball, dressed in
a sparkly ice-blue cape and an enormous
sparkly blue top hat.

"It's me!" he announced.

To Rachel and Kirsty's amazement,
the audience roared with laughter. Mimi
drew in her breath sharply.

"Look what's around his neck," she
exclaimed. "My magical smiley-
face pendant!"

Jack Frost strutted across the stage, put his hands on his hips and glared at the watching fairies.

"Knock knock!" he bellowed.

"Who's there?" they replied.

"Fairy," said Jack Frost.

"Fairy who?" the audience chanted.

"*Fairy* pleased to meet you!" he shouted.

Again the fairies squealed with
laughter, clutching their sides and rolling
about on the grass.

"How many fairies does it take
to screw in a light bulb?" Jack Frost
demanded. "Three! One to screw it in,
one to cast a pesky spell on it, and one to
flutter about being annoying."

The fairies were crying tears of
laughter now. Jack Frost was on a roll.

"What do you call a fairy who's always
agreeing with you? Fairy Nuff! Get it?"

"These jokes aren't even *jokes*," said
Kirsty. "How can the other fairies think
they're so funny?"

"It's because he's wearing the magical
pendant," Mimi replied in a whisper. "As
long as he has it, every time he tries to be
funny, people will laugh. The only reason

I'm not laughing is because the pendant belongs to me. It can't be used to trick me."

"Why did the fairy cross the road?" Jack called out. "Because the silly thing forgot she could fly!"

The laughter was deafening, and a smug grin had appeared on Jack Frost's face.

"We have to get that pendant back *now*," said Rachel. "I can't bear to hear our friends laughing at these unfunny, nasty jokes."

Suddenly, Kirsty grabbed Rachel's arm in excitement.

"I've got an idea!" she whispered.

Pie Pandemonium

"Jack Frost thinks that he's the most amazing comedian ever," Kirsty said. "Let's pretend to be fans! He's so conceited that he's bound to believe us. We'll ask for his autograph, and then Mimi can unhook the pendant while he's signing."

"Great idea!" said Rachel.

The two friends started pretending to splutter with laughter, and they rushed onto the stage, swerved around the goblin assistants and dashed over to Jack Frost.

"Your jokes are the funniest I've ever heard!" Kirsty gushed.

"Please, *please* could we have your autograph?" begged Rachel.

Jack Frost's smug smile grew even smugger. But then he looked at the audience and shook his head.

"I have a duty to *all* my fans," he said, putting his hand over his heart. "I must continue with the show, and you are interrupting me. Come back for an autograph later."

"But we can't wait," said Kirsty.

"Of course you can," said Jack Frost. "I'm the funniest, best and most handsome act in the whole of Fairyland *and* the human world. You will wait until *I* am ready!"

He gave them both such a shove that they went skidding back into the wings, landing in a tangled heap of arms, legs and wings. Mimi helped them up and they all peered out onto the stage again.

One of the
goblin assistants
was doing
a wobbly
pirouette. As he
spun around, he
pulled a sparkly
blue wig from
behind the glitter
ball. The other goblin
did a little jog, then
dived into the glitter ball
and pulled out an enormous blue bow tie.

"Your outfit, sir," squawked the first
goblin.

Jack Frost snatched the wig and the
bow tie, and quickly put them on. Then
he swept a deep bow to the audience,
who were almost hysterical with laughter.

"Mr Twinkle's bow tie is much better," said Rachel.

"So are his jokes," Kirsty added. "Remember the cream pie?"

She and Rachel grinned at each other, and then their eyes widened. They had exactly the same idea at exactly the same time!

"Mimi, can you magic up a tray of cream pies?" Rachel asked.

Mimi just smiled and waved her wand. Instantly, a huge tray of whipped-cream pies appeared in Rachel's arms.

"Come on," she said to Kirsty. "We have to make Jack Frost *want* to give us the pendant!"

Rachel and Kirsty ran onto the stage and put the tray of pies down between them. Then they each picked one up and took aim.

"Three … two … one … FIRE!" Kirsty whispered.

WHOOSH! WHOOSH! Two cream pies flew through the air. *SPLAT!* One knocked Jack Frost's wig off. *SPLODGE!* The other was a direct hit right on his sharp nose, which

poked through the paper plate.

Jack Frost yanked the plate off and clawed at his face, wiping great blobs of cream out of his eyes and flicking them onto the stage. The fairies in the audience were beside themselves, laughing even harder than before. They obviously thought that this was supposed to happen.

"Stop laughing!" Jack Frost snarled through gritted teeth. "This isn't part of my show! I'm the joke-*maker*, not the joke, you miserable pack of weedy wing flappers!"

The laughter stopped at once. Jack Frost turned to Rachel and Kirsty, his eyes blazing with anger. They stepped a little closer together. It made them feel braver to be beside each other.

"Give me those pies," Jack Frost hissed. "If anyone around here is going to be throwing cream pies, it'll be me, not a pair of spindly fairies."

"You can't have them," said Rachel, trying not to let her voice wobble. "They belong to us, just like that pendant you're wearing belongs to Mimi."

"Give them to me!" Jack Frost hollered. But the friends shook their heads.

"You can only have them if you give Mimi back her pendant first," said Kirsty. Jack Frost's eyes narrowed, and then he turned his head towards the audience. The girls could tell that he wanted more laughter and applause.

"They really liked it when you threw those pies," he muttered. "All right, if you insist. You can have the silly pendant – as long as I can throw some pies!"

A Lot of Laughter

Jack Frost took the pendant from around his neck and held it out to Rachel. She took it and flew to the wings, where she handed it straight to Mimi.

The Laughter Fairy hugged Rachel, and then darted onto the stage as Kirsty handed the tray of cream pies to Jack Frost. A grin spread across his face and he pointed to his goblin assistants.

"You!" he yelled. "Stand still!"

"Not likely!" squealed the goblins, darting sideways.

Cream pies flew through the air as the goblins dodged and weaved around the stage. Soon the stage floor was white and slippery with cream, and the goblins and Jack Frost were skating around in the mixture, staggering as they tried to keep their balance. The Music Fairies, who were in the audience, struck up a merry tune and soon everyone was in fits of laughter. The goblins were doing everything they could to avoid being splatted, from climbing the stage curtains to limbo dancing under low-flying pies.

"Stand still!" Jack Frost shrieked again.

There was just one pie left. He started to chase the bigger goblin, but then he trod on one of the sticky, splatted pies on the stage floor, and skidded on it.

"HEEELLLLP!" Jack Frost cried, as he careered across the stage.

The pie he was holding flew high up into the air, and came down with the biggest *SPLAT* yet – right on top of his head! He landed with a bump on his bottom, and the whole audience roared with laughter.

Rachel and Kirsty hurried over to help Jack Frost to his feet. At first he looked furious, but as the applause rose and the audience cheered, he started to smile. Standing beside Rachel, Kirsty and the two goblin assistants, he took several bows. The fairies rose to their feet and clapped their hands above their heads.

Jack Frost was looking happier than Rachel and Kirsty had ever seen him. He bowed again and again, soaking up the cheers and the applause. When the girls gave a final wave to the audience and headed back into the wings, the goblin assistants were still trying to drag Jack Frost off the stage.

"Please come," Rachel heard one of them begging. "We really need to get your costume in the washing machine before the cream pies stain it!"

Rachel and Kirsty grinned as they shared a hug with Mimi. Her pendant was safely hanging around her neck.

"Thank you both," said Mimi, beaming. "I am so happy to have my smiley-face pendant back, and it's all thanks to you. I must send you home now, but I want

69

you to know that I will never forget how you have helped me. Friends for ever!"

The three of them shared a hug, and then Mimi waved her wand. There was a shimmer of fairy dust, and the laughter of the fairies faded. Rachel and Kirsty blinked, and saw that instead of the garden of the Fairyland Palace, they were once again standing beside the fountain in Rainspell Park. The laughter of the fairies had been replaced by the laughter of their friends in the Summer Friends Club.

Mr Twinkle was telling jokes, and Jen, Ginny and all the children were holding their sides and roaring with laughter. Even the goblins beside the fountain started giggling when Mr Twinkle turned and squirted them with his water flower.

"It looks as if things are back to normal, thank goodness," said Kirsty, squeezing Rachel's hand.

Mr Twinkle finished with an amazing trick where he made his hat disappear, and then reappear on Lara's head! Then, amid cheers, laughter and claps, he rode his unicycle away down the path, waving goodbye.

"This has been the most fun day so far!" said Oscar, as they headed back across the park to the tepee.

Lara bent her knees and did a funny walk, setting everyone off into giggles again. Oscar started telling jokes, and Rachel and Kirsty glanced back at the fountain. The goblins were still beside it, watching the children and looking sad.

"No one should be left out," said Rachel, waving to the goblins. "Come and join us!"

Cheering up immediately, the goblins leapfrogged across the grass to catch up with the children. They tripped over their big feet and tumbled around, head over heels. Giggling, the other children joined in, leapfrogging over the goblins and each other. Their laughter rang out across the park, and Rachel and Kirsty exchanged a special smile.

"I'm so happy," said Kirsty.

"I know," said Rachel. "Now only Clare the Caring Fairy's magical object is missing. I hope we can get it back!"

"We will," said Kirsty determinedly.

"We won't stop until all friendships are as happy as ours!"

The End

Now it's time for Kirsty and Rachel to help...

Clare the Caring Fairy

Read on for a sneak peek...

It was a beautiful summer's afternoon on Rainspell Island. Rachel Walker pulled shut the door of the Sunny Days Bed and Breakfast and skipped down the steps. Her best friend Kirsty Tate was waiting for her on the path, and their parents had already started walking towards the park.

"I'm really looking forward to this barbecue," said Rachel. "I'm starving!"

"I think the hot weather makes us hungrier than usual," said Kirsty with a grin. "Just *thinking* about burgers is making my stomach rumble!"

Rachel laughed and reached out to

hold Kirsty's hand.

"This has been one of the best holidays ever," she said, as they hurried to catch up with their parents. "I can't believe that we're going home tomorrow."

"Holidays on Rainspell always go too fast," said Kirsty.

The two girls shared a secret smile. Rainspell Island was the place where they had met and become best friends, and where they had had their first adventures with the fairies.

"It's a great idea to celebrate the last day of the Summer Friends Club with a barbecue," said Mr Walker, with a twinkle in his eye. "I love barbecues!"

At the start of their holiday, the girls had joined the Summer Friends Club, a holiday play scheme for children who were staying on the island. Now they had reached the end of their stay, it was time to say goodbye to all their new friends.

"Although it has been a bit harder to make friends than I thought it would be," Kirsty said to Rachel.

"I agree," Rachel replied. "It's all because of mean Jack Frost and his goblins. They've caused a lot of mischief."

Read Clare the Caring Fairy to find out what adventures are in store for Kirsty and Rachel!

Competition!

The Friendship Fairies have created a special competition just for you!

Collect all four books in the Friendship Fairies series and answer the special questions in the back of each one.

What does Mr Twinkle like to throw on people's faces?

_ _ _

Once you have all four answers, take the first letter from each one and arrange them to spell a secret word! When you have the answer, go online and enter!

We will put all the correct entries into a draw and select a winner to receive a special Rainbow Magic Goody Bag featuring lots of treats for you and your fairy friends. The winner will also feature in a new Rainbow Magic story!

Enter online now at www.rainbowmagicbooks.co.uk

Calling all parents, carers and teachers!
The Rainbow Magic fairies are here to help
your child enter the magical world of reading.
Whatever reading stage they are at, there's
a Rainbow Magic book for everyone!
Here is Lydia the Reading Fairy's guide to
supporting your child's journey at all levels.

Starting Out

(1) Our Rainbow Magic Beginner Readers are perfect for first-time readers who are just beginning to develop reading skills and confidence. Approved by teachers, they contain a full range of educational levelling, as well as lively full-colour illustrations.

Developing Readers

(2) Rainbow Magic Early Readers contain longer stories and wider vocabulary for building stamina and growing confidence. These are adaptations of our most popular Rainbow Magic stories, specially developed for younger readers in conjunction with an Early Years reading consultant, with full-colour illustrations.

Going Solo

(3) The Rainbow Magic chapter books – a mixture of series and one-off specials – contain accessible writing to encourage your child to venture into reading independently. These highly collectible and much-loved magical stories inspire a love of reading to last a lifetime.

www.rainbowmagicbooks.co.uk

"Rainbow Magic got my daughter reading chapter books. Great sparkly covers, cute fairies and traditional stories full of magic that she found impossible to put down" – Mother of Edie (6 years)

"Florence LOVES the Rainbow Magic books. She really enjoys readi[ng]
Mother of Florence (6 years)

The Rainbow Magic Reading Challenge

Well done, fairy friend – you have completed the book!
This book was worth 5 points.

See how far you have climbed on the **Reading Rainbow**
on the Rainbow Magic website below.

The more books you read, the more points you will get,
and the closer you will be to becoming a Fairy Princess!

How to get your Reading Rainbow
1. Cut out the coin below
2. Go to the Rainbow Magic website
3. Download and print out your poster
4. Add your coin and climb up the Reading Rainbow!

There's all this and lots more at
www.rainbowmagicbooks.co.uk

You'll find activities, competitions, stories, a special
newsletter and complete profiles of all the
Rainbow Magic fairies. Find a fairy with your name!